The People vs. Mona
A Musical Mystery Screwball Comedy

Book by
Patricia Miller and Jim Wann

Music and Lyrics by
Jim Wann

ISBN 978-0-573-66028-3   Printed in U.S.A.   #17824

RENTAL MATERIALS

An orchestration consisting of **Bass, Guitar, Vocal Score, and Piano Conductor Score** will be loaned two months prior to the production ONLY on the receipt of the Licensing Fee quoted for all performances, the rental fee and a refundable deposit.

Please contact Samuel French for perusal of the music materials as well as a performance license application.

IMPORTANT BILLING AND CREDIT REQUIREMENTS

All producers of *THE PEOPLE VS. MONA must* give credit to the Author of the Play in all programs distributed in connection with performances of the Play, and in all instances in which the title of the Play appears for the purposes of advertising, publicizing or otherwise exploiting the Play and/or a production. The name of the Author *must* appear on a separate line on which no other name appears, immediately following the title and *must* appear in size of type not less than fifty percent of the size of the title type. In addition the folowing billing *must* be followed:

(Name of Producer)
presents
"THE PEOPLE VS. MONA"

<table>
<tr><td align="center">Music and Lyrics by
Jim Wann</td><td align="center">Book by
Patricia Miller and Jim Wann</td></tr>
</table>

THE PEOPLE VS. MONA was presented by the Pasadena Playhouse (Sheldon Epps, Artistic Director) in a world premiere production, March 12, 2000. The book co-author was Ernest Chambers, and the cast was as follows:

JIM SUMMERFORD/GUITARS. .Scott Waara
MONA MAE KATT/SOUSAPHONE. . . . . .Kelli Maguire
MAVIS FRYE/GUITAR/MANDOLIN. . . . . .Maggie Hollinbeck
JUDGE RIGGS/BLIND WILLY/KEYBOARDS. . . . . .William Thomas, Jr.
BAILIFF/CORONER/EUPLE R. PUGH/PATEL/
        FLUTE/ACCORDION. . . . . .Joe Joyce
TISH/REV. PURIFY/
        COURT RECORDER/PERCUSSION. . . . . . .Michele Mais
OFFICER BELL/CLERK/BASS/UKULELE. . . . . .Ritt Henn

The production was directed by Paul Lazarus, with music arrangements by Pete Snell, vocal arrangements by Brad Ellis, scenic design by Lawrence Miller, lighting design by Michael Gilliam, costume design by Nancy Konrardy, sound design by Tim Metzger, and casting by Julia Flores. The production stage manager was Cari Norton, and the stage manager was Tim Burt.

THE PEOPLE vs. MONA was presented by the York Theatre Company (James Morgan, Artistic Director) on March 30, 2008, in association with JAY Records, London. An original cast album was recorded April 1 - 2, 2008. The cast was as follows:

JIM SUMMERFORD . . . . Marc Kudisch
MONA MAE KATT . . . . Natalie Toro
MAVIS FRYE . . . . Christiane Noll
JUDGE JORDAN/REV. PURIFY . . . . m . . . . . Lillias White
TISH THOMAS/BLIND WILLY . . . . Marcie Henderson
OFFICER BELL/KITTEN . . . . Ron Raines
BARTENDER/DR. BLOODWEATHER/EUPLE R. PUGH/
        PATEL/BAILIFF/KITTEN. . . . . Omri Schein
MACK McGNAT/BASS/UKULELE/CLERK . . . . Ritt Henn
MIKE McGNAT/GUITAR/TAMBOURINE . . . . Dan Weiss
NAT McGNAT/KEYBOARDS/COURT RECORDER . . . Bob Gustafson

The production was directed by Annette Jolles and the musical directors were Rob Mikulski and Bob Gustafson, with music arrangements by Ritt Henn.

THE PEOPLE vs. MONA was presented by Ground UP Productions (Kate Middleton, Artistic Director) as an Equity Approved Showcase at the Abingdon Theatre, in New York City, July 14 - August 4, 2007. The cast was as follows:

JIM SUMMERFORD . . . . Richard Binder
MONA MAE KATT . . . . Mariand Torres
MAVIS FRYE . . . . Karen Culp
JUDGE JORDAN/REV. PURIFY . . . . Natalie Douglas
TISH THOMAS/BLIND WILLY . . . . Marcie Henderson
OFFICER BELL/KITTEN . . . . David Jon Wilson
BARTENDER/DR. BLOODWEATHER/EUPLE R. PUGH/
          PATEL/BAILIFF/KITTEN . . . . Omri Schein
MACK McGNAT/BASS/UKULELE/CLERK . . . . Ritt Henn
MIKE McGNAT/GUITAR/TAMBOURINE . . . . Jason Chimonides
NAT McGNAT/KEYBOARDS/COURT RECORDER . . . . . . Dan Bailey

The production was directed by Kate Middleton, stage managed by Devan Hibbard, and the musical director was Rob Mikulski, with set & lighting designed by Travis McHale, costume design by Elisa Richards, choreography by Jill Gorrie, sound design by Duane McKee and Randy Morrison, and music arrangements by Ritt Henn.

The authors wish to thank everyone involved in these productions, and also Marilyn Stasio, Helene Blue, John Yap, Ron Gwiazda, Amy Wagner, Donald Maass, and our wonderful friends at Samuel French. Further, we thank everyone who encouraged *MONA* from her beginnings in 1999:

The ASCAP Musical Theatre Workshop, Los Angeles, directed by Stephen Schwartz and Michael Kerker; ASCAP at the Berkshire Theatre Festival; Ernest Chambers, Lisa Patterson, and Merv Griffin in Los Angeles; and MARS Theatricals in New York.

The authors would also like to thank the theatrical organizations who produced *THE PEOPLE VS. MONA* after Pasadena and before New York: Theatrical Outfit, Atlanta; Chattanooga Theatre Center; Visalia Players, Visalia, CA; Theatrical Outfit/Alliance Theatre, Atlanta; and San Diego State University. These organizations, along with Pasadena, Ground Up Productions and the York Theatre, generously allowed nearly constant rewriting, creation of new characters, plotlines, dialogue, scenes, songs, and musical arrangements over a ten-year period.

THE PEOPLE VS. MONA is a musical for 7 actor-singers, some playing more than one role, and 3 musicians, who also play minor roles. Multi-cultural casting is strongly urged, to reflect the New South. The ensemble could be made larger, if desired, by casting one actor to play each witness, thus creating a kind of chorus.

Accompaniment shall be piano, guitar, and bass (the "McGnats").

SETTING

The Frog Pad, a friendly watering hole in the south Georgia town of Tippo. Much loved over many years, its walls show the passage of time in music posters, old instruments, quirky signs and the like. Flexible design allows the Frog Pad to become the courtroom and other locales, and its denizens to become courtroom characters.

TIME

The present.

THE THREE MAIN CHARACTERS

JIM SUMMERFORD, Defense Attorney, Narrator – Easy going Southern gentleman

RAMONA MARÍA "MONA MAE" KATT, Defendant – Third-generation American Latina, Frog Pad Owner; Down-to-earth, naturally sexy, passionate and idealistic

MAVIS FRYE, Prosecutor – Ambitious, upscale, chic

THE FOUR ADDITIONAL COURTROOM CHARACTERS

JUDGE ELLA JORDAN – Smart, no-nonsense

BAILIFF – Regular guy/gal

COURT RECORDER – Regular guy/gal

CLERK – Regular guy/gal

WITNESSES FOR THE PROSECUTION

TISH THOMAS, Journalist – Tippo's culture maven

GORDON BELL, Traffic Officer – Sensitive cop

DR. THEODORE BLOODWEATHER, Coroner – Serious professional

KATT'S KITTENS – Backup singers

WITNESSES FOR THE DEFENSE

EUPLE R. PUGH – Elderly attorney, local hero

"BLIND WILLY" CARTER, Street Singer – Street-smart

RAFSANJANI PATEL, Motel Proprietor – New Southerner, assimilated & proud

REVEREND ROSETTA PURIFY – Dynamic, sincere, a true believer

How the roles were cast in the New York City productions:

1. Jim Summerford (male)
2. Mona Mae Katt (female, Latina)
3. Mavis Frye (female)
4. Judge Jordan/Rev. Purify (female, African American)
5. Tish Thomas/Blind Willy (female, African American)
6. Officer Bell, Kitten (male)
7. Bartender, Dr. Bloodweather, Euple R. Pugh, Patel, Bailiff, Kitten (male)
8. Mack McGnat, Bass, Ukulele, Clerk (male)
9. Mike McGnat, Guitar, Tambourine (male)
10. Nat McGnat, Keyboards, Court Recorder (male)

This is not the only way the roles can be combined; that said, this template worked extremely well. And it's not the only formula for achieving a multicultural cast. That's up to each production. Any actor of any heritage can potentially play any role. The important thing is that the ensemble be multicultural to reflect the fact that the New South is multicultural.

PLAYING STYLE: HIGH ENERGY, FAST-PACED. LAUGHTER AND APPLAUSE ARE CERTAINLY HIGH AMONG THE GOALS.

YET THE CHARACTERS ARE ROOTED IN THE REALITY OF THEIR WORLD, NOT TO BE CONDESCENDED TO IN ANY WAY BY THE ACTORS OR DIRECTOR.

FOR THE SHOW TO SATISFY ON ALL LEVELS, THE ACTORS MUST BELIEVE IN THE REALITY OF THEIR CHARACTERS, HOWEVER HUMOROUSLY THEY ARE CREATED, TO GIVE THE AUDIENCE A FULL MEASURE OF SATISFACTION IN THE SPECIAL WORLD OF TIPPO AND THE FROG PAD.

MUSICAL NUMBERS

(SINGERS in parentheses)

ACT ONE

1.   TIPPO (JIM, McGNATS, COMPANY)
2.   KEEP THE FROG PAD ALIVE (MONA, COMPANY)
3.   KEEP, KEEP/HEAR YE/WHO WEARS THE ROBE?/GLAD GLAD GLAD (CLERK, JUDGE, MONA, COMPANY)
4.   EUPLE R. PUGH (JIM, COMPANY)
5.   DO YOU? (CLERK, TISH)
6.   THE BIG MEOW (TISH, MONA, KITTENS)
7.   OFFICER BELL'S TURN (OFFICER BELL, CLERK)
8.   WORK WITH ME (JIM, MONA, McGNATS)
9.   LOCKDOWN BLUES (MONA, JIM, McGNATS, MAVIS)
10. DOES THE PROSECUTION REST? (JUDGE, MAVIS)
11. RIVERBOAT CASINO GAMBLING (MAVIS, COMPANY)
12. RIVERBOAT CASINO GAMBLING/Reprise (MAVIS, MONA, JIM, COMPANY)

ACT TWO

13. EUPLE R. PUGH/LEGENDARY LITIGATOR (PUGH, COMPANY)
14. BLIND WILLY (BLIND WILLY, COMPANY)
15. MARCHING THRU TIPPO (MONA, COMPANY)
16. YOU DONE FORGOT YOUR BIBLE (REV. PURIFY, MAVIS, COMPANY)
17. PARTNER (MONA, JIM)
18. A REAL DEFENSE (JIM, COMPANY)
19. SPOOKY MEMORIES (VARIOUS)
20. THE CONFESSION (???)
21. COME ON DOWN TO TIPPO (ALL)

PROLOGUE

PRE-SHOW: Recorded music of southern roots flavors starts playing over the house system at half-hour, at the right level to encourage the audience to talk among themselves.

As the audience enters, the members of the band assemble on stage, hook up their instruments, adjust mics (if any), check props, and acknowledge audience in the front rows in a natural, friendly way.

At "Places," CAST enters randomly and settles in the Frog Pad while the pre-show music still plays. This takes no more than a minute. (Don't drag it out and don't invent dialogue.)

MACK MCGNAT *begins a walking bass figure (Music in, Opening Underscore) ; the pre-show music fades down, and* **JIM** *speaks.*

JIM. Friends, have you ever been to Tippo? Tippo, Georgia that is. Not as old as Savannah or as new as Atlanta – it's a small town in between, with a tale to tell…

McGNATS, COMPANY. *(variously)* Tell it, Jim! Yes sir! Tell 'em all about it!

JIM. I'm Jim Summerford, Tippo attorney – I welcome you all to the Frog Pad, the musical heart of Tippo…home to armadillos and blues, gators and gospel, gnats and mack-gnats – that's our band, The McGnats –

*(**McGNATS** acknowledge, play riffs; full band is playing by now; **CAST** acknowledges **McGNATS**.)*

JIM. Uh huh! We're in South Georgia now, has everybody got a fan?

Hold up your fans, will you?

You can move 'em around –

You can fan yourselves –

Let's have everybody fanning themselves at once!

Ah, would you look at that.

That is a wonderful sight.

You can stop now.

These fans come to you courtesy of Murchesson's Funeral Home in Tippo. "When you can no longer feel the heat – " *(Music out.)*

McGNATS. "You will be ready for Murchesson's!" *(Music in, #1.)*

JIM. Our story begins in the Frog Pad, on a night, not long ago, when we were having a little libation and trying to solve one small problem:

ACT ONE

SONG #1: TIPPO

JIM.

> TIPPO IS A TAPPED-OUT TOWN

JIM, COMPANY.

> YEAH, TIPPO IS A TAPPED-OUT TOWN
> IF WE DON'T GET UP SOMEHOW,
> WE GONNA STAY DOWN

JIM.

> OUR ECONOMY HAS GONE WITH THE COTTON MILL

JIM, COMPANY.

> YES, OUR FUTURE HAS FLOWN OVER THE HILL
> WE ALL PASS AROUND THE SAME FIVE-DOLLAR BILL

JIM.

> NOW, OTHER PLACES THIS SMALL
> HAVE A BOOKSTORE, A CONCERT HALL
> RIGHT NEXT DOOR TO

JIM, COMPANY.

> AN ART EXHIBIT!

JIM.

> TIPPO AIN'T SO BAD

McGNATS.

> WE LOVE THE FROG PAD

JIM.

> BUT ALL OUR SYMPHONIES
> TEND TO SOUND LIKE

JIM, McGNATS, COMPANY.

> "RIBBIT!"

JIM.

> WHAT ARE WE GONNA DO ABOUT TIPPO?

JIM, COMPANY.

> CAN'T JUST SET AND WATCH OUR FIELDS TURN BROWN
> THE NEW SOUTH IS HAPP'NIN', SO HOW DO WE TAP IN?

JIM.

WE CAN'T GO ON BEIN' A TAPPED-OUT TOWN

COMPANY.

TIPPO IS A TAPPED-OUT,

JIM, COMPANY.

TIPPO IS A TAPPED-OUT,
TIPPO IS A TAPPED-OUT TOWN

JIM.

NOW, UP THE ROAD IN CARY
THEY'RE ALMOST CULINARY
WITH BARBECUE AND NEW WINERIES
PULLED PORK AND PULLED CORKS
PULL 'EM IN FROM NEW YORK
CARY'S RE-INVENTED

JIM, COMPANY.

TASTY AS YOU PLEASE –
BUT WHAT ARE WE GONNA DO ABOUT TIPPO?
WE'RE AS TAPPED-OUT AS LAST WEEK'S BEER

JIM.

WE NEED SOME FIZZ, THE PROBLEM IS

JIM, COMPANY.

NOTHING EVER HAPPENS HERE

*(PHONE rings. "**BARTENDER**" answers.)*

BARTENDER. Frog Pad. Hey, Tish – what's the dish? He what? She what?

*(To **COMPANY**)* C.C. Katt's been murdered! *(Music out.)*

JIM, COMPANY. No!

BARTENDER. And they're after Mona!

McGNATS. *Our* Mona?

JIM. I thought she was getting married to C.C. Katt!

BARTENDER. *(Shrugs helplessly)* Catch you later, Tish –

COMPANY. Murder – Mona – Holy Cow!

*(**MONA** enters on "Holy Cow!" Distant siren sounds.)*

MONA. Hola, my little angels!

COMPANY. Mona! Run!

MONA. No, no, I've got to face the music – but first – I need a lawyer –

JIM. You got one!

MONA. Thanks, Jim – McGnats, you're in charge – everything the same, you know the drill, you practically live here –

McGNATS. We do live here. But Mona, what happened? *(Music in, #2.)*

MONA. First, a wedding. (**McGNATS** *play chord*) Second, a honeymoon. *(Another chord)* And now – *(Sound of sirens)* The police!

SONG #2: KEEP THE FROG PAD ALIVE

COMPANY. *(spoken)*

OH, MONA! WHAT CAN WE DO?

MONA.

SOMETIMES THERE'S JUST NOTHIN' YOU CAN DO
ABOUT A BAD DAY
BAD THINGS THEY SAY COME IN THREES
AND WHEN THE FIRST TWO
HAVE GOT YOU ON YOUR KNEES
YOU NEED A PLACE TO COME TO

COMPANY. *(sung)*

RIBBIT

MONA.

SOME FRIENDS TO BELONG TO

COMPANY.

RIBBIT

MONA.

CAUSE THE NEXT BAD THING TO HAPPEN TO ME
WE MIGHT AS WELL PUT IT UP ON THE MARQUEE

MONA, COMPANY.

COMING SOON, THE PEOPLE VERSUS MONA

MONA.

IF YOU WANT MY HOPE TO SURVIVE

MONA, COMPANY.

ALL THROUGH THE PEOPLE VERSUS MONA

MONA.

PROMISE ME YOU'LL KEEP THE FROG PAD ALIVE
EIGHTY-EIGHT SUMMERS, FALL, WINTER, SPRINGS
THE FROG PAD'S ALWAYS BEEN

THE PLACE THAT SINGS
LIKE A FROG IN MY FAMILY TREE
THESE OL' WALLS, TO ME THEY TALK

COMPANY.

RIBBIT

MONA.

HOW MY GRANDDADDY WALKED THE WALK

COMPANY.

RIBBIT

MONA.

BUSING TABLES TO MAKE HIS RENT
WHEN ROOSEVELT WAS THE PRESIDENT.

MONA, COMPANY.

ROOSEVELT, THE POOR MAN'S FRIEND!

(Sirens – Pounding on Door)

COMING UP, THE PEOPLE VERSUS MONA

MONA.

IF YOU WANT MY HOPE TO SURVIVE

MONA, COMPANY.

ALL THROUGH THE PEOPLE VERSUS MONA

MONA.

PROMISE ME YOU'LL KEEP THE FROG PAD ALIVE!

(Pounding: "Come Out, Mona! We know you're in there! Come out or we're coming in!")

Quiet! We're praying in here! *(Gathers Frog Pad folks around her)*

MONA. (**COMPANY** *OOH AAH*)

WE PULLED OURSELVES UP
BY OUR BOOTS…
SO SEND SOME RAIN
DOWN ON OUR ROOTS…
MAY WE GROW
MAY WE THRIVE…

(More pounding – "That's enough praying! Come on out right now!")

Dear Lord –

AND KEEP THE FROG PAD,
KEEP THE FROG PAD ALIVE – SING IT WITH ME!

MONA, COMPANY.

KEEP THE FROG PAD,
KEEP THE FROG PAD ALIVE!

MONA.

TELL EVERYBODY, Y'ALL!

MONA, COMPANY.

COMING NOW, THE PEOPLE VERSUS MONA

MONA.

IF YOU WANT MY HOPE TO SURVIVE

MONA, COMPANY.

ALL THROUGH THE PEOPLE VERSUS MONA
KEEP THE FROG PAD, KEEP THE FROG PAD ALIVE!

MONA.

TELL EVERYBODY, Y'ALL!

MONA, COMPANY.

KEEP THE FROG PAD, KEEP THE FROG PAD ALIVE!

(More pounding, shouting)

MONA. I'm coming, I'm coming!

MONA, COMPANY.

KEEP THE FROG PAD, KEEP THE FROG PAD ALIVE!

(Song ends.)

MONA. *(Over applause)* Remember now!

SONG #3: KEEP KEEP/HEAR YE/WHO WEARS THE ROBE?/GLAD GLAD GLAD

COMPANY. *(as **MONA** exits and scene changes)*

KEEP, KEEP THE FROG PAD ALIVE
KEEP, KEEP THE FROG PAD ALIVE
KEEP, KEEP THE FROG PAD ALIVE
KEEP, KEEP THE FROG PAD ALIVE
KEEP, KEEP THE FROG PAD ALIVE
KEEP, KEEP THE FROG PAD ALIVE

(Sing through scene change, and more quietly under HEAR YE as tempo slows.)

SCENE: The Tippo Courtroom

CLERK, (COMPANY).
HEAR YE (KEEP KEEP THE FROG PAD ALIVE)
HEAR YE (KEEP KEEP THE FROG PAD ALIVE)
THE PEOPLE VERSUS MONA MAE KATT
THE TOLERABLY HONORABLE ELLA JORDAN
PRESIDING

BAILIFF. All rise!

(If audience is slow to rise)

All rise *now*!

(If audience is still slow)

Come on people, go with me on this – *(Lively 2-beat vamp;* **BAILIFF** *gestures for audience to rise.)* All rise! Thank you!

(New feel; **JUDGE** *enters and puts on her Robe.)*

BAILIFF. Please be seated.

JUDGE.
IS THE PROSECUTION READY?

MAVIS.
YES, YOUR HONOR –

JUDGE.
IS THE DEFENSE READY?

JIM.
YES, YOUR HONOR!

JUDGE.
IS EVERYBODY READY?

JIM, MAVIS, CLERK, COMPANY.
YES, YOUR HONOR!

JUDGE. Listen up!
YOU'RE IN MY COURT, YOU GOT TO FOLLOW MY RULES
I TELL YOU RIGHT NOW, I DON'T SUFFER NO FOOLS
NO HOOCHIE, NO COOCHIE –
WHO WEARS THE ROBE?

JIM, MAVIS, CLERK, COMPANY.
YOU DO, JUDGE!

JUDGE.
WHO WEARS THE ROBE?

JIM, MAVIS, CLERK, COMPANY.
YOU DO, JUDGE!

JUDGE.
ONE MORE TIME!

JIM, MAVIS, CLERK, COMPANY.
YOU DO, JUDGE!!!

JUDGE. The Clerk will read the charges.

CLERK. Ramona María "Mona Mae" Katt, you are hereby charged with the murder of your husband, Clyde Cloyd "C.C." Katt. How do you plead?

JIM. Your Honor, on behalf of my client –

MONA. I can speak for myself, Jim!
C.C. KATT…WHAT WERE THOSE VOWS WE SAID?
TIT FOR TAT…NOW I'M ALIVE AND YOU'RE DEAD
(Full Tempo and Energy)
YES, I'M ALIVE AND YOU'RE DEAD DEAD DEAD
I'M ALIVE, ALIVE AND YOU'RE DEAD

JIM. Mona –

MONA.
I'M GLAD GLAD GLAD YOU'RE DEAD DEAD DEAD

JIM. Mona – !

MONA.
GLAD GLAD GLAD, GLAD GLAD GLAD –

JIM. Mona!!!! *(Music out.)* The plea is Not Guilty, Your Honor.

MAVIS. Well, that about wraps it up. Let's throw the book at her and we can all go home.

JUDGE. *(Gavels)* Ms. Frye, may I remind you that we have a little concept in this country called "innocent until proven guilty."

MAVIS. Oh, that.

JIM. Mavis Frye. Miss Tippo High School, Vanderbilt Law Review…and my fiancée. I've tried 29 cases against Mavis, plea-bargained 12, lost the other 17. Believe me, I'm due.

JUDGE. Your Opening Statement, please.

MAVIS. Your Honor, ladies and gentlemen, the prosecution will prove that the defendant, Mona Mae Katt, had been married to her husband, C.C. Katt, for exactly ten hours when she arrived at the Turk Street office of Star Studio, interrupted his usual dinner of pizza and a bottle of Yoo-Hoo Chocolate Drink and, after an argument that escalated into violence, clubbed him to death with Exhibit A – her custom-made, personalized and glitterized Stratocaster guitar!

(**BAILIFF** *holds up GUITAR, ludicrously bent out of shape.*)

JIM. *(To AUDIENCE)* At this point, a murmur went through the courtroom. Could you folks give us a murmur, please?

(AUDIENCE murmurs – **JUDGE** *pounds gavel.)*

JUDGE. Order! Order! Counselor, continue.

MAVIS. And Mona Mae Katt committed this heinous crime while she was wearing Exhibit B, her wedding dress – as you can see, splattered with Yoo-Hoo.

(**BAILIFF** *holds up DRESS, on a hanger, with huge chocolate stain.*)

JIM. *(To AUDIENCE)* An audible gasp was heard in the courtroom.

(**JIM** *indicates someone in audience to give an AUDIBLE GASP.)*

Thank you.

JUDGE. Mr. Summerford? For the Defense?

JIM. Your Honor, the defense will acknowledge that Mona Mae Katt had the motive, the opportunity, and the murder weapon – but personally, I don't think she did it.

JUDGE. Counselor, that is the worst Opening Statement I've ever heard in all my years on the bench.

JIM. I was just being honest, Your Honor.

JUDGE. In a court of law? Where did you go to law school?

JIM. Euple R. Pugh. School of Law.

SONG #4: EUPLE R. PUGH

JIM, COMPANY.

> HAIL, HAIL, EUPLE R. PUGH!
> LEGENDARY LITIGATOR EUPLE R. PUGH!
> WE HONOR THE LAW SCHOOL NAMED FOR YOU
> IN DOWNTOWN TIPPO

JIM, (COMPANY).

> ONE FLIGHT UP FROM THE TURK STREET GRILL (DOO)
> FULL SEMESTER FOR A HUNDRED DOLLAR BILL (DOO)
> I CAN SMELL THOSE ONIONS STILL (DOO)

JIM, COMPANY.

> HAIL, ALL HAIL EUPLE R. PUGH!
> HAIL, HAIL, EUPLE R. PUGH!
> WALK-UP LAW SCHOOL EUPLE R. PUGH!

JIM, (COMPANY).

> THE ONLY ONE I COULD GET INTO – (AAH)

JIM, COMPANY.

> HAIL, EUPLE R. PUGH –
> HAIL, ALL HAIL EUPLE R. PUGH!

> *(Song ends.)*

MAVIS. *(to* **JIM***)* I love honest lawyers. It makes for faster convictions.

JIM. What's your hurry? I thought you enjoyed beating the pants off me.

MAVIS. I'm moving on to bigger britches. It's my destiny. Have a button, honey.

JIM. "Mavis For Mayor." You never told me about this –

MAVIS. I have now! And as soon as this Mona foolishness is over we'll get married. It's time and I'm booking the church.

JIM. Now, we don't want to rush into things, Mavis.

MAVIS. Trust me, Jim, an 8½-year engagement is not rushing into things!

JUDGE. I'm deeply touched by this romantic interlude, but let's get a witness up here.

MAVIS. Your Honor, The Prosecution calls Tish Thomas to the stand.

SONG #5: DO YOU?

CLERK.
> DO YOU
> SWEAR TO
> TELL THE TRUTH,
> THE WHOLE TRUTH,
> AND NOTHING BUT THE TRUTH, SO HELP YOU GOD?

TISH.
> I DO
> I DO
> I DO, I DO, I DO, I DO, I DO *(Song ends, no applause.)*

MAVIS. Ms. Thomas, what is your profession?

TISH. I am a journalist. I write a column on Tippo Culture, it's a very short column.

MAVIS. Did you cover the wedding of C.C.Katt and his Killer Bimbo?

JIM. Objection!

JUDGE. Sustained!

MAVIS. Is that the dress you saw the defendant wearing at her wedding?

TISH. Yes.

MAVIS. Will you tell the court what happened when you attempted to cover the honeymoon at the Harmony Hotel?

TISH. I was about to knock on the door of the Bridal Suite, when C.C.burst out, and Mona yelled, "I'll kill you, I swear, I'll kill you!" Then C.C. crept off, on his little Katt feet.

MAVIS. Let the jury note that the Defendant threatened to kill her husband on her wedding day, and, you heard it, she's glad glad glad, glad glad glad, glad glad glad he's dead. Your witness.

JIM. Ms. Thomas, is that dress one of a kind?

TISH. No, everybody in town has one – the Mayor's wife, the Doctor's wife, even Mavis. I did not buy one, because I do not like to meet myself coming and going.

JIM. So you cannot be certain that this is the Defendant's dress?

TISH. I cannot.

JIM. Now, Ms. Thomas, isn't it true that C.C. Katt had affairs with many women?

MONA. And he wasn't gonna quit! That's what he told me that day –

JIM. Mona, sit down!

MONA. Well, it's true.

JUDGE. Order in the court –

MONA. But, Judge – we hadn't been married a full day and he was already Kattin' around!!

JUDGE. Mona!! *(to* **JIM***)* Proceed.

JIM. In fact, isn't it true that Katt had a harem of backup singers known as the Kittens and that you were once one of them? Did you not perform under the name "Bustin' Buttons?"

JUDGE. You were "Bustin' Buttons"?

TISH. YES! Yes, I admit it. I'm a woman with a past. *(Music in, #6.)* I sang. I danced. I was his little kitten, but I wasn't the first or the last.

SONG #6: THE BIG MEOW

TISH, KITTENS.
> MEOW – MEOW, MEOW, MEOW
> MEOW – MEOW, MEOW, MEOW

TISH.
> KATT'S GOT SLEEPY BEDROOM EYES
> PEARLY WHITES AND TIGHT-FITTIN' LEVI'S
> FEDORA DOWN OVER ONE EYEBROW

TISH, KITTENS.
> AIN'T HE THE BIG, AIN'T HE THE BIG,
> AIN'T HE THE BIG MEOW

TISH.
> KATT MAKES SURE YOU DON'T IGNORE HIM
> HIS SLINKY WALK DO HIS TALKING FOR HIM

HE LEADS YOU TO HIS LAIR,
WHERE THE KITTENS KOWTOW
TISH, KITTENS.
AIN'T HE THE BIG, AIN'T HE THE BIG,
AIN'T HE THE BIG MEOW
TISH.
YOU'RE THE ONLY ONE
KITTENS.
THAT'S HIS JIVIN' SONG
TISH.
SO YOU COME UNDONE
TISH, KITTENS.
WHEN HE COMES ON STRONG
TISH.
SO SMITTEN YOU DON'T FEAR
KITTENS.
HE'S TAKIN' ALL YOUR MONEY
TISH.
PURRIN' IN YOUR EAR
TISH, MONA.
"TRUST ME, HONEY"
TISH. But, ladies –
TISH, KITTENS.
NEVER TRUST A MAN
TISH.
WHOSE PERFUME IS STRONGER
TISH, KITTENS.
NO, NEVER TRUST A MAN
TISH.
WHOSE EYELASHES ARE LONGER
TISH, KITTENS.
NEVER TRUST A MAN
TISH.
WHO WEARS TALL POMPADOURS
TISH, KITTENS.
NEVER TRUST A MAN
WHOSE HAIR IS HIGHER THAN YOURS

KITTENS.   TISH.

 MEOW, MEOW

 MEOW, MEOW

 MEOW MEOW

 MEOW, MEOW   These are my boys —

 MEOW, MEOW   cost me a fortune,

 MEOW MEOW

 MEOW MEOW   but they're worth it!

 MEOW, MEOW

TISH.

 THE BIG MEOW MADE US ALL A WRECK

KITTENS.

 WRECK, WRECK!

TISH.

 MADE US WANT TO GET OUR CLAWS ON HIS NECK

KITTENS.

 NECK, NECK!

TISH.

 HE WAS SATAN

KITTENS.

 LATE DATIN'

TISH.

 ALL THE DEVIL WOULD ALLOW

TISH, KITTENS.

 AND THE DEVIL'S GOT HIM NOW

 AIN'T HE THE BIG, AIN'T HE THE BIG,

 AIN'T HE THE BIG MEOW

 AIN'T HE THE BIG, AIN'T HE THE BIG,

 AIN'T HE THE BIG MEOW

TISH.

 I DON'T MISS HIM AT ALL

TISH, KITTENS.

 ME – OW!

 ME – OW!

 ME – OW!!!

 (Song ends.)

JIM. So, there are many women who would like to see Katt dead, including you, Ms. Thomas.

MAVIS. Objection!

JIM. No further questions. *(To* **MONA***)* Just tell me you didn't go upside his head, smashin' and bashin'.

MONA. Sounds like what a Killer Bimbo would do.

JIM. I objected to Killer Bimbo –

MONA. The jury still heard it from your fiancée and I don't like it. I might just run for Mayor myself. "Killer Bimbo Takes On Bigger Britches, Cuts Her Down To Size."

JIM. That'll be a colorful campaign, and you won't have to worry about security – you'll be in maximum security, cause you wouldn't give your lawyer any help.

JUDGE. *(gavels)* Ms. Frye, bring out your next witness please.

MAVIS. I now call to the stand Officer Gordon Bell of the elite Tippo Parking Violations Unit.

SONG #7: OFFICER BELL'S TURN

*(***CLERK*** begins to play "DO YOU?" but BELL interrrrupts.)*

BELL.

> I DO!
>
> *(stage whisper)* Hey Mona.

MAVIS. Thank you. Officer, the parking meters in the vicinity of Star Studio are legally operational until midnight, is that correct?

BELL.

> THAT IS CORRECT.

MAVIS. And on the night of July 1st, tell us about a certain car you saw there.

BELL.

> I WROTE A TICKET FOR A PINK CADILLAC
> PARKED ILLEGALLY ON TURK STREET
> NEAR THE OFFICE OF C.C. KATT
> WHO ELSE WOULD OWN A CAR LIKE THAT?
> THE BIG HONCHO,
> I HAD A SONG
> I WANTED TO SING FOR HIM

MAVIS. Yes, but what time was it?

BELL.

> THE TIME ON THE TICKET THAT FATEFUL NIGHT
> WAS TEN-OH-TWO P.M.!

MAVIS. I would ask the Court to note that time – ten-oh-two p.m. Your witness.

JIM. Officer, did you actually see anyone in the car?

BELL.

> NO – BUT MONA ALWAYS DROVE THE KATTMOBILE.

JIM. That was not the question.

BELL.

> I'M JUST TRYING TO BE HELPFUL...HELPFUL...

JIM. Officer Bell, you have a wonderful voice. Doesn't he, ladies and gentlemen? Are you an actor in your spare time?

BELL.

> I HAVE APPEARED AS 'CURLY' IN THE TURK STREET
> PLAYHOUSE PRODUCTION OF 'OKLAHOMA.'

JIM. And your beat takes you past Star Studio frequently?

BELL.

> YES...

JIM. Did you ever go in and record anything?

BELL.

> TO RECORD MY 'CURLY' IS MY LIFE'S MISSION
> BUT C.C. KATT NEVER WOULD GRANT ME
> AN AUDITION

JIM. And did you hate him for that? Enough to kill him? Sing out, Curly!

MAVIS. Objection! Officer Bell's voice has nothing to do with this case.

JUDGE. Sustained. Strike those last riffs.

> (**CLERK** *plays descending riff.*)

JIM. Is there anything else you'd like to say to this court?

BELL. (*to* **COURT RECORDER**) "D" Flat –

> (*sung*) POOR KATT IS DEAD, POOR C.C. KATT IS DEAD

JUDGE. (*Cutting him off*) Step down, step down!

BELL. (*stage whisper*) Bye Mona.

MAVIS. I now call to the stand the County Coroner, Dr. Theodore Bloodweather. (*Music in.*)

CLERK.
DO YOU . . . SWEAR TO . . . *(Music out under* **CORONER.***)*

CORONER. I do, but I don't. Sing, that is. My God, you do not want to hear me sing.

MAVIS. That's all right, Doctor. Tell the Court how many autopsies you have performed on dead people.

CORONER. All my autopsies have been on dead people.

MAVIS. Good, good. Now just tell us, what was the cause of death? *(encouraging him)* In your own words.

CORONER. I'd like to point out to you, and every other lawyer that asks me that question, I don't have any of my own words. If I were to use my own words, they would sound like nonsense. So if it's all right with you, I'll go on speaking the English language and refrain from confusing the Court.

MAVIS. It must be mighty stressful working with the dead, that's all I can say. Could you determine the time of death?

CORONER. Near ten p.m.

MAVIS. Let the court note – ten p.m., within two minutes of the time already established. Your witness!

JIM. Dr. Bloodweather, tell us how you determine the time of death.

CORONER. Corpses cool at a certain rate. Katt's body was 97.1 degrees at midnight, meaning he died two hours earlier.

JIM. Isn't it true that the heat could have kept the body warm for hours? That in fact he could have died any time that evening?

MAVIS. Objection! Mr. Summerford, the doctor does not need a lesson on dead bodies.

JIM. I think he does. Because the doctor happens to be a dentist. Yes, not an MD, but a DD.

CORONER. DDS!

JIM. *(To AUDIENCE)* I had hit a nerve. *(If they groan)* Nice groan.

MAVIS. But Your Honor, any competent dentist can determine time of death by the condition of the corpse's gums!

JUDGE. Gums. I've never heard that one before.

MAVIS. Your Honor, Dr. Bloodweather was elected Coroner by the good people of Tippo County.

JIM. With the financing of C.C.Katt! As you may recall, Dr. Bloodweather ruled suicide in the suspicious death of one of Katt's kittens, a Ms. Rhonda Zippers!

CORONER. Rhonda's gums were blue –

JIM, JUDGE. Blue???

JUDGE. Objection sustained! Mr. Summerford, the doctor's not on trial here. The witness may step down.

CORONER. *(Exiting, to* **JIM***)* And she was not always his kitten.

MONA. Oh Jim, that was really good!

(Gives **JIM** *a hug & kiss – they hold embrace.)*

MAVIS. Objection!

JUDGE. Sustained. What did I tell you people? No hoochie, no coochie. I'll have no hoochie-coochie in my courtroom! (**JIM** *and* **MONA** *pull apart.)* Let's take a five minute recess.

(All but **JIM** *and* **MONA** *exit or fade into background.)*

JIM. *(To AUDIENCE)* Something just happened…When Mona hugged me, I could feel a conflict of interest –

MONA. Jim, I feel something I haven't felt in a long time – hope!

JIM. Hope – esperanza!

MONA. Sí –

JIM. Yes?

MONA. Sí!

JIM. Sí! Yes!!! You tutored me in Spanish –

MONA. At Tippo High!

JIM. I hadn't thought of that in years. I liked you, but you were younger – you ran with a different crowd.

MONA. Yes, the crowd picking onions in the fields.

JIM. But weren't you the first Freshman to be Head Majorette?

MONA. Sí! Marching with the band made me feel like I belonged – and the Frog Pad makes everyone feel they belong. Tippo needs the Frog Pad, Jim!

JIM. And I really need to win this trial. So tell me, where were you?

MONA. Jim…we can work together, can't we?

JIM. Absolutely! It's just that I'll defend you better if I know the facts.

MONA. Everybody else already knows the facts. "Busted on her wedding day. She boffed him, then she offed him. He went from a shagging to a toe-tagging" –

JIM. Tabloid headlines are not facts.

MONA. Thank you, Jim! I knew you'd understand! *(Hugs* **JIM** *again. Music in, #8. They dance close together.)*

JIM. *(To AUDIENCE)* She hadn't answered my question. That bothered me…everything about her was bothering me.

SONG #8: WORK WITH ME

JIM.

THEY SAY YOU STAYED OUT HALF THE NIGHT
WHAT YOU WERE DOIN', IT JUST WEREN'T RIGHT
WORK WITH ME, MONA – WORK WITH ME, MONA
WORK WITH ME, MONA, HELP ME SEE THE LIGHT

MONA.

THEY SAY YOUR FIANCÉE'S A-COUNTIN' ON YOU
TELL ME, JIMMY, WHAT YOU'RE GONNA DO
WORK WITH ME, JIMMY – WORK WITH ME, JIMMY
WORK WITH ME, JIMMY, MAYBE I'LL WORK WITH YOU

*(***JIM*** and ***MONA*** dance.)*

McGNATS.

WORK WORK, BABY CAN YOU WORK?
WORK WORK, BABY CAN YOU WORK?
WORK WORK, BABY CAN YOU WORK?
CAN YOU WORK WITH ME?

JIM, MONA.

DON'T NEED A WORKING HYPOTHESIS
WHEN PROOF WILL MAKE ME SURE

DON'T NEED A ROCKET SCIENTIST
TO TAKE MY TEMPERATURE

JIM.

CAN I TRUST YOU TO TRUST ME?

MONA.

IN A BIND, ARE YOU BOUND OR FREE?

JIM.

WORK WITH ME, MONA

MONA.

WORK WITH ME, JIMMY

JIM.

WORK WITH ME, MONA

MONA.

WORK WITH ME, JIMMY

JIM, MONA.

WE'LL SEE WHAT WE WILL SEE

McGNATS.	JIM, MONA.
WORK WORK, BABY CAN YOU WORK?	
	WORK, WORK, WORK
WORK WORK, BABY CAN YOU WORK?	
	WORK, WORK, WORK

McGNATS.

WORK WORK, BABY CAN YOU WORK?

JIM, MONA.

CAN YOU WORK WITH ME?

(Song ends.)

JUDGE. *(Gavels)* Court is back in session.

JIM. *(To AUDIENCE)* Mavis went on to introduce another fourteen witnesses – the cleaning woman who found the body, the rookie investigating officer who threw up on the body, the lab technician who declared the Yoo-Hoo on the dress to be a match for the Yoo-Hoo in the bottle Katt was drinking from and so on. And worst of all, Mavis established that Mona's guitar and her dress were found at the crime scene.

JUDGE. That's all we have time for today. Court will reconvene tomorrow morning.

MONA. *(exiting)* Esperanza, Jim.

JIM. Esperanza...

MAVIS. Jim....let's go someplace and negotiate a little candlelight dinner and wine. Then we'll adjourn to my chambers – I'll be the party of the first part, you can be the party of the second part and we can get our parts together.

JIM. I'm always the party of the second part. Why can't I be the party of the first part?

MAVIS. I'm the party of the first part. That's what we negotiated. Your part always comes second to my part.

JIM. Mavis, I think I just need to relax and hang out with my buddies at the Frog Pad.

MAVIS. Well then, I suggest you enjoy it while you can. *(exits)*

JIM. *(To AUDIENCE)* What did she mean by that? I worked on my notes for a while, then I walked outside. It was getting dark and the courthouse lawn was deserted. From up above, where the jail was, came the sound of singing – her sound.

SONG #9: LOCKDOWN BLUES

MONA.
WHEN THAT OLD EVENING SUN GOES DOWN
AND BRINGS THE DAY TO ITS KNEES
AND DARKNESS FALLS ON TIPPO
IT'S STILL NINETY-SEVEN DEGREES
AND THE HEAT BUILDS UP IN THE OL' CELLBLOCK
TILL IT'S TOO HOT TO TOUCH THE BARS
AND YOUR ONE AND ONLY WINDOW
IS A PRISON FOR THE STARS

WHEN THEY LOCK YOU DOWN IN TIPPO JAIL
YOU'LL SWEAR YOU'RE BORN TO LOSE
AND ALL YOU DO IS MOAN AND WAIL
THE LOCKDOWN BLUES
AND YOUR HEART IS BURSTING WITH A SECRET
YOU JUST CAN'T FACE

YOU'RE FALLING IN LOVE WITH YOUR LAWYER
AND HE'S NEVER WON A CASE
YO-DE-LAY-EE-AY, NEVER WON A CASE…

JIM. I needed a drink. I walked to the Frog Pad by way of Turk St…visitors were out in front of Star Studio, taking pictures…someone was playing "Glow Worm" on a trombone, it floated from a window of the Harmony Hotel…a shipment of laurel plants stood by a wall outside the Coroner's building…curious…laurel doesn't grow around Tippo…in the sidewalk cement, someone had written "I heart Rhonda Zippers" with a little drawing of a zipper…Tippo was more mysterious than I had ever dreamed. I headed on into the Frog Pad and there were the McGnats. *(Music out under next line.)* Hey, Mike, hey Mack, hey Nat.

McGNATS. Hey Jim. How's Mona?

JIM. They can lock her down, but they can't stop her singing.

McGNATS. I miss her. Mona's the best owner the Frog Pad's ever had. What'll happen to us if she's found guilty?

JIM. Just stay positive. She can feel our positive thoughts. *(Music in.)*

MONA.

WHEN THEY LOCK YOU DOWN IN TIPPO JAIL
YOU'LL SWEAR YOU'RE BORN TO LOSE
AND ALL YOU DO IS MOAN AND WAIL
THE LOCKDOWN BLUES
AND YOUR HEART IS BURSTING WITH A SECRET
YOU JUST CAN'T FACE
YOU'RE FALLING IN LOVE WITH YOUR LAWYER

McGNATS.

AND HE'S NEVER WON A CASE

MONA.

YO-DE-LAY-EE-AY, NEVER WON A CASE…

JIM.

I DON'T WANT TO LOSE

MAVIS. *(In a tub with bubbles – could be a cutout – reading "The Fountainhead")*

IT'S HER HE MUST REFUSE

MONA, JIM, MAVIS.
> LOCKDOWN BLUES!
> *(Song ends.)*

JIM. *(To AUDIENCE)* The next day dawned early.

CLERK. Court is back in session. *(Music in, #10.)*

JUDGE. Ms. Frye, do you have any more witnesses?

MAVIS. No, Your Honor –

SONG #10: DOES THE PROSECUTION REST?

JUDGE.
> DOES THE PROSECUTION REST?

MAVIS.
> I DO, I DO

JUDGE.
> DOES THE PROSECUTION REST?

MAVIS.
> I DO, I DO

JUDGE.
> ONE MORE TIME!

MAVIS.
> I DO, I DO
> I DO, I DO, I DO, I DO *(Music out.)*
> Have a button, Judge – you're gonna be swearing me in soon! I've got the answer for Tippo's future! Riverboat Gambling!

JIM. Excuse me? There's no river here to put a riverboat in!

MAVIS. We've got a pond – and the Frog Pad is sitting on it – it'll make the perfect dock for the Casino, when it's torn down.

JIM. Tear down the Frog Pad for a riverboat casino?! You'll change the whole character of Tippo!

MAVIS. *(Music sneaks in, #11.)* Who's gonna care when Mawmaw and Pawpaw and all their little buddies start pulling the slot handles? We're talking jobs, and a tax base – The New South is all about New Money. Wake up and smell the Starbucks, Jim!

SONG #11: RIVERBOAT CASINO GAMBLING

MAVIS.

I HAVE A VISION FOR MY TAPPED-OUT TOWN

COMPANY.

YOU DO? YOU DO, YOU DO, YOU DO?

MAVIS.

A BRAND-NEW BLUEPRINT

FOR RICHES AND RENOWN

COMPANY.

YOU DO? YOU DO, YOU DO, YOU DO?

MAVIS.

I SEE A SKYLINE TURNING NEON

IT'S TURNING ME ON

AND BEFORE I'M THROUGH

YOU'RE GONNA CHEER

COMPANY. *(spoken)*

YEOW!

MAVIS.

WHO'S GOT IT ALL IN GEAR?

COMPANY. *(sung)*

YOU DO! YOU DO, YOU DO, YOU DO!

SHE HAS A VISION, THIS TOWN IS HERS

MAVIS.

BRIGHT LIGHTS, BIG TIPPO

COMPANY.

ON TOP'S THE POSITION SHE PREFERS

MAVIS.

OTHERWISE, I FEEL ZIPPO

AND TO RAISE MY CAMPAIGN MONEY SOON

I'LL HAVE A HONEYMOON WITH THE POWERS THAT BE!

NOTHING IS FREE, SO WHY NOT BUY ME?

COMPANY.

WE DO! WE DO, WE DO, WE DO!

MAVIS, COMPANY.

RIVERBOAT CASINO GAMBLING

NEVER MIND WE DON'T HAVE A RIVER

WE'LL BUILD OUR CASINO AND A SIX-LANE ROAD

THEN TAP INTO THE MOTHER LODE, LODE, LODE
TAP INTO THE MOTHER LODE

(Next section with Tap Steps)

MAVIS.

NOW TAP IN –
GOODBYE TO TAPPED-OUT –
WE'LL BRING A GLITZY TOURIST TRAP IN –
I'VE GOT IT ALL MAPPED OUT –
VEGAS-STYLE BROADWAY, WHOLESOME SLEAZE
LOW-PAID TALENT AND A HIGH-TICKET SQUEEZE
LOTS OF LIP-SYNCHING TO MUSIC MACHINES
SMOKE BOMBS, LASER LIGHTS, VIDEO SCREENS

MAVIS, COMPANY.

RIVERBOAT CASINO GAMBLING
YOU'LL FORGET YOU EVER HAD A FROG PAD
INSIDE THE ARTIFICIAL ATMOSPHERE
YOU CAN BE ANYWHERE BUT HERE, HERE, HERE
YOU CAN BE ANYWHERE BUT HERE

MONA. Objection, her vision is a nightmare! Doesn't anybody care about the Frog Pad and Tippo?

MAVIS.

NO GUITARS, NO PIANO
TONY SOPRANO WILL WELCOME YOU
I'M TIRED OF HAND-TO-MOUTH,
I WANT THE NEW SOUTH!
I DO! I DO, I DO, I DO!
I DO, I DO, I DO, I DO, I DO!

COMPANY.

SHE DO SHE DO, SHE DO SHE DO
SHE DO SHE DO, SHE DO SHE DO
SHE DO SHE DO, SHE DO SHE DO

MAVIS.	**COMPANY**
I DO!!!	SHE DO!!!

(Song ends.)

MONA. Jim, we can't let that happen!

JIM. You own the Frog Pad, she can't take it away from you unless you're convicted.

MONA. I'm not guilty. I didn't do it.

JIM. So where were you, and who were you with, when your husband was killed? Are you protecting someone?

MONA. I wish I could tell you.

JIM. Mona, if you're convicted, the Frog Pad will go straight from the auction block to a dock for this Casino, and that will be the end of Tippo as we know it.

MONA. The Frog Pad is our music – and it's the oldest juke joint in the state of Georgia – it's our roots, and it's what we should build on! My Granddaddy worked there as a busboy when he first came to this country. Then my Daddy ended up owning it. Talk about the American Dream – Tear down the Frog Pad? Now that's a capital offense!

JIM. I'm with you, but you've got to help me. Tell me where you were, please Mona…I hate to bring this up, but they still use Ol' Sparky in this state, do you understand? The priest and his Bible…Psalm 23…the last meal…the last mile…Dead Mona Walking…Dead Mona Walking…

MONA. Okay, okay, okay! I was at the Santa Claus Motel!

JIM. The Santa Claus Motel?!

MONA. With Euple R. Pugh.

JIM. *(Stunned)* Euple R. Pugh! *(Music in, #11a.)*

COMPANY.

    HAIL, HAIL, EUPLE R. PUGH! *(Music out.)*

JIM. He's a hundred years old!

MONA. Ninety-six.

JIM. What were you doing with him on your wedding night?

MONA. Getting legal advice.

JIM. Your Honor, I request a recess – I want to call a witness who can prove beyond a shadow of a doubt that my client could not have committed the murder!

MAVIS. Objection! This is obviously a delaying tactic.

JUDGE. Overruled.

JIM. *(To CLERK)* Subpoena Euple R. Pugh!!

COMPANY.
> HAIL . . . H . . . (**JIM** *cuts them off.*)

JUDGE. Get the witness here in fifteen minutes and I'll allow it. *(gavels)*

JIM. Now we've got a fighting chance!

MAVIS. Make the most of your fifteen minutes, Bimbo, because the future is mine.

MONA. Al contrario! The future belongs to everyone. Peace, Mavis.

MAVIS. War, Mona!

SONG #12: RIVERBOAT CASINO GAMBLING (Reprise)

MAVIS.	**MONA.**
RIVERBOAT CASINO GAMBLING	THE FROG PAD!
YOU'LL FORGET	
YOU EVER HAD	WE'VE GOT TO KEEP
A FROG PAD	THE FROG PAD
I'M NOT GIVING UP	ALIVE
8 AND ½ YEARS	SINGING
STAYING SINGLE	PLAYING
IS THE SUM OF ALL FEARS	HISTORY AND
NO KILLER BIMBO	JOY
CAN KNOCK ME OFF MY PERCH	HERITAGE
A MAYOR NEEDS A MATE	LOVE
AND I'M BOOKING THE CHURCH	NO ONE CAN DESTROY

MAVIS.

JIM, YOU'LL SAY "I DO" RIGHT ON CUE

MONA.

JIM, YOU KNOW WHAT'S REAL AND TRUE

MAVIS.

THE PREACHER AND THE RING

MONA.

I WANT TIPPO TO SING

JIM.

AND I WANT EUPLE R. PUGH

MAVIS, MONA, JIM.

I DO, I DO, I DO, I DO, I DO!

COMPANY.

THEY DO THEY DO, THEY DO THEY DO
THEY DO THEY DO, THEY DO THEY DO
THEY DO THEY DO, THEY DO THEY DO

MAVIS, MONA, JIM.	**COMPANY.**
I DO!!!	THEY DO!!!

(Song ends.)

END ACT ONE

ACT TWO

*ENTR'ACTE (****McGNATS*** *play an instrumental reprise of "Riverboat Casino Gambling" and acknowledge applause.)*

JIM. *(To AUDIENCE)* Welcome back, everybody! Did you see those demonstrators carrying signs? "Mona Must Pay" and "Let My Mona Go". Fifteen for and fifteen against. Tippo is split down the middle. Who knows where this will wind up? Oh, there's a familiar face. Morning, Officer Bell!

BELL. *(spoken)* Oh, what a beautiful morning.

JIM. Yes indeed. What are you up to?

BELL. Those demonstrators got here last night. I brought them pepperoni pizza and Yoo-Hoo – like Katt's last meal.

JIM. That was awfully nice of you.

BELL. *(sung, a cappella)*
I'M JUST TRYING TO BE HELPFUL, HELPFUL.

JIM. *(To AUDIENCE)* You know, that's just the kind of thing that makes Tippo so special. Everybody looks out for one another.

BELL. Tell Mona hey.

JIM. And now I had a client to look out for – I headed into the Courtroom. Hi, Mona – Officer Bell says hey.

MONA. Hey. Look at this book from the jail library – "Handbook For Poisoners"…You can make cyanide poison right in your own kitchen. You boil the leaves of some plant, it's amazing what you can learn in jail.

JUDGE. *(Gavels)* Court is back in session.

MONA. We've got to win, Jim –

JIM. We're gonna win. The train of justice is finally pulling into Summerford Station. *(Makes train sound)* "Woo Woo!" I call to the stand Euple R. Pugh!

SONG #13: EUPLE R. PUGH/LEGENDARY LITIGATOR

COMPANY.

HAIL, HAIL, EUPLE R. PUGH!
LEGENDARY LITIGATOR EUPLE R. PUGH!

PUGH. (*To* **MONA**) Hey, Sweet Pea. (*kisses her hand*)

MONA, (COMPANY).

I KNEW I COULD COUNT ON YOU (OOO)
EUPIE

COMPANY. "EUPIE?"

PUGH. That's right! EUPIE!!!

(*Cajun-style count-off*)

1-2-3-4!

PUGH.

LEGENDARY, LEGENDARY, LEGENDARY, HI!

COMPANY.

LEGENDARY, LEGENDARY, LEGENDARY, HI!

PUGH.

LITIGATOR, LITIGATOR, LITIGATOR, HO!

COMPANY.

LITIGATOR, LITIGATOR, LITIGATOR, HO!

PUGH.

MASTER OF THE COURTROOM SWITCHEROO!

COMPANY.

MASTER OF THE COURTROOM SWITCHEROO!

PUGH.

EUPLE R., EUPLE R., EUPLE R. PUGH!

COMPANY.

EUPLE R., EUPLE R., EUPLE R. PUGH!

JUDGE. Mr. Pugh, will you be sworn?

CLERK, COMPANY.

DO YOU SWEAR TO TELL THE TRUTH,
THE WHOLE TRUTH, AND NOTHING BUT THE TRUTH,
SO HELP YOU GOD?

PUGH. (*raises right hand*)

I DO

(*cough wheeze*)

I DO
(*cough wheeze*)
I DO

JIM. Take it easy Mr. Pugh, just please tell us exactly where you were and who you were with at ten p.m. on the night of July 1st?

PUGH.

JULY ONE AT TEN O'CLOCK I'M

COMPANY.

JULY ONE AT TEN O'CLOCK I'M

PUGH.

HAVING MYSELF A LARGE TIME!

COMPANY.

HAVING MYSELF A LARGE TIME!

PUGH.

BOWL OF CHIPS AND A TALL CORONA

COMPANY.

BOWL OF CHIPS AND A TALL CORONA

PUGH.

IN THE MOTEL WITH MY ARM AROUND – (*Music out.*)

JIM. Mr. Pugh . . . Mr. Pugh . . . Mr. Pugh . . .

(**PUGH** *does not respond.* **JIM** *touches* **PUGH**'s *arm; he droops*)

Mona, your alibi just bought the farm.

(*Music in.* **PUGH** *is lowered to the floor by* **CAST** *members.*)

COMPANY.

FAREWELL, EUPLE R. PUGH.

(*"GOD" LIGHT appears from on high, upstage. Leaving* **CAST** *members in position as though still cradling him,* **PUGH** *rises and walks "into the light" as song ends.*)

MONA. This town sure is gonna miss him.

JIM. Your Honor, it's obvious that Mr. Pugh was going to say his arm was around Mona. Corona – Mona –

MAVIS. Objection! There are many things that rhyme with Corona – Fiona, Jonah, Wynona, Roshashona . . .

JIM. That's not a name!

JUDGE. Sustained. This is pure conjecture. The jury will disregard the rhyming of the deceased.

MAVIS. Well, Jim, your train of justice jumped the track again. "Woo Woo!" Let's see, that's derailment number eighteen . . .but who's counting?

MONA. Jim, I told you the truth, you believe me don't you?

JIM. I don't know what to believe! You've done some mighty peculiar things. Marrying that slimebag C.C. Katt, then spending your wedding night with a 96-year-old man. Why?

MONA. C.C. Katt double-crossed me on my wedding day. I married him because he promised me that he would help me save the Frog Pad from the casino developers. But he was working with them all along. That's why I went to Eupie.

JIM. You knew about the casino back then?

MONA. Oh, yes, C.C. told me all they needed to do was to get the right person in the Mayor's office. Then they could do whatever they wanted, the schmucks. *(glares at Mavis)* Rhymes with bucks!

JUDGE. *(gavels)* Counselor will proceed. Do you have a *live* witness?

JIM. Yes, Your Honor. His name is William Carter –

MAVIS. Objection!

JUDGE. Already?

MAVIS. This witness is notorious, Your Honor. He's a street-singing, rhyme-making throwback to muddy water, moonshine, and love in vain.

JUDGE. Overruled, Ms. Frye. I have an affinity for street-singing, rhyme-making throwbacks to muddy water, moonshine, and love in vain – Take it, Mr. Carter!

SONG #14: BLIND WILLY

WILLY.
THEY CALL ME BLIND WILLY
'CAUSE I CAN'T SEE
YEAH, THEY CALL ME BLIND WILLY

COMPANY. (*spoken*)

WHY?

WILLY.

'CAUSE I CAN'T SEE

COMPANY. (*spoken*)

OH.

WILLY.

BUT ALL MY OTHER SENSES
STILL WORKIN' FOR ME
MY NOSE KNOWS EVERY SMELL ON THE STREET
I CAN SNIFF OUT GARDENIA AT TWENTY FEET
THERE'S A KIND OF MUSK THAT FLOATS BY AT DUSK
ON A GOOD DAY I CAN TELL
ALL THE NUMBERS OF CHANEL
WELL, THEY CALL ME BLIND WILLY

(**WILLY** *veers toward edge of stage, but is steered back.*)

COMPANY. (*spoken*)

WHOA!

BLIND WILLY.

I GOT TWENTY-TWENTY SCENT
YEAH, I'M BLIND WILLY
I GOT TWENTY-TWENTY SCENT
BABY, TOUCH ME WITH YOUR PERFUME
IT'S LIKE A FINGERPRINT

JIM. Mr. Carter, you sing on Turk Street next to Star Studio, correct?

WILLY. Uh-huh.

JIM. Were you there on the night in question?

WILLY. From eight till late.

JIM. And since you're legally blind –

WILLY. In my good eye –

JIM. You depend on your highly developed sense of smell –

WILLY. I call it "the scent-illator" –

JIM. Did you pick up any aromas around the entrance to Star Studio that night?

MAVIS. Objection! How can we be sure this man smells what he says he smells? (*Music out.*)

JUDGE. Why don't we let the People decide?

WILLY. Works for me! How 'bout it, People! I'll smell y'all, one at a time! *(Music in, slower.)*

MAVIS. Eeeww!

(**WILLY** *goes into AUDIENCE if possible.*)

HARD SALAMI FROM THE DELI BOX
OLD SPICE, AND VERY OLD GYM SOCKS
FRESH PESTO, THEN A GARGLE WITH SCOPE
ERNO LASZLO SEA MUD SOAP
BEENIE WEENIES, SELSUN BLUE
KIWI POLISH, OOH –
CHECK THE BOTTOM OF YOUR SHOE
COCKER SPANIEL, POWDER FOR THE FLEA
OH, IT'S MR. DANIEL'S, FROM LYNCHBURG,

(music returns to original tempo)

TENNESSEE!
JACK BLACK, WATER BACK!
Am I right or am I right! Listen –

MAVIS. This is nothing but a stunt, and I object!

JUDGE. Overruled! Witness will answer the question.

WILLY. What was the question?

JIM. Did you pick up any aromas in front of Star Studio around ten p.m.?

WILLY. The savory, the stenchy, the fragrant, the funky, I got 'em all on file. *(Taps his nose)*

JIM. Thank you, Mr. Carter – let the record show, any number of fragrant and funky characters went by Star Studio that night, and any one of them could have crept in and killed the Katt. Your witness.

MAVIS. All right, Mr. Carter, let's say you were smelling up a storm in front of the studio that evening. Did any particular smell stand out – more than the others – perhaps a woman's perfume?

WILLY. Yeah, come to think of it. I call it "Eau de No Mercy."

IT STARTED FROM THE HOTEL, A SUBTLE WHIFF
BOTH SWEET AND HOT, LIKE A SAXOPHONE RIFF

THEN COMING CLOSER, ON HIGH HEELS CLICKIN'
A SCENT TO START A DEAD MULE KICKIN'
THE APOGEE OF THE INVISIBLE
WHEN SHE PASSED ME BY, I CAUGHT IT IN FULL
THE OVERTONES, THE UNDERTONES
I WAS WIGGY FOR WEEKS FROM THE PHEROMONES!

JUDGE. The pheromones?!

WILLY. Unsmellable smells that trigger attraction in the brain. Didn't none of y'all study Science at Tippo High? Pheromones are the ultimate scent-sation!

MAVIS. Mr. Carter, do you get that same scent-sation in this courtroom?

WILLY. Oh, indeed I do. *(He smells his way over to* **MONA.***)* The perfume is coming from – right here!

COMPANY. *(sung)*

MONA!!!

MAVIS. No further questions.

WILLY. Wait, you didn't let me finish – and right over there. *(Pointing toward* **MAVIS***)*

COMPANY. *(sung)*

MAVIS!!!

JIM. *(To AUDIENCE)* At this revelation, an "ooo" swept through the audience like a wave. (**JIM** *gestures to AUDIENCE)* Mr. Carter, what does this mean?

WILLY. Mr. Summerford, I call 'em like I smell 'em.

SO, STEP RIGHT UP, PUT A NICKEL IN MY HAT
HOW 'BOUT A QUARTER, I'D LIKE THAT
SIX BITS, BUY ME SOME GRITS
IF YOU THROW DOWN A DOLLAR,
YOU'LL MAKE ME WANNA HOLLER
'CAUSE I'M TWENTY-TWENTY, DON'T YOU SEE
MY SCENT-SATION LIKE EYESIGHT TO ME!
YEAH!

WILLY, COMPANY.

BLIND WILLY!

WILLY. Thank you! Thank you!

(Song ends.)

JIM. "Eau de No Mercy"…Mavis, it's so you.

MAVIS. I was testing the witness, of course. I knew all along it was Mona's perfume. I just wanted to see if Willy knew.

JIM. Uh-huh. (**MAVIS** *walks away.*)

MONA. What do you think, Jim? Was she at the studio that night?

JIM. I wonder…were you?

MONA. I walked by Mr. Carter on my way to the Santa Claus.

JIM. Did anyone who can *see*, see you at the motel?

MONA. Yes! The owner checked us in! Mr. Patel! He can be my alibi!

JIM. *(To AUDIENCE)* Suddenly it was Christmas in July – thirty minutes later my witness, Mr. Rafsanjani Patel –

PATEL. Call me Johnny!

JIM. – was being sworn in.

PATEL. I am always telling the truth, good buddy!

JIM. Mr. Patel, how long have you operated the Motel?

PATEL. Nearly about six year.

JIM. How did you come to be in the hospitality business?

PATEL. I am coming from India at the age of seventeen, and I am learning two things. Number one: Patel and Motel are going together very well in the South.

JIM. Yes indeed. What else?

PATEL. Football is my life! Oh yes! I have one year at Tippo High and also attending University of Georgia. How 'bout them dawgs!

JIM. Hunker down, hairy dog!

PATEL. I am hunkering down, you hairy dog!

PATEL, JIM. Uga! Uga! Woof! Woof! Woof! Woof! Woof! *("Uga" is the Bulldog mascot; his name is pronounced "Uh-ga" with a hard "g".)*

JIM. Mr. Patel –

PATEL. And to heck with Georgia Tech! Yes!

JIM. Yes! Now, Mr. Patel, turning your attention to the night of July 1st –

PATEL. Yes –

JIM. Do you recall registering the defendant and Mr. Pugh that evening?

PATEL. I surely do.

JIM. You're sure it was Mona Mae?

PATEL. Oh, yes – she is head Majorette my year at Tippo High, marching at halftime –

JIM. Yes – I remember –

PATEL. Because I love football, I am going to every game. The stands are empty, then at halftime – not one seat left! She is being bigger than football!

JIM. I can see it now.

PATEL. I am seeing it too, good buddy!

SONG #15: MARCHING THROUGH TIPPO

COMPANY.

MARCHING THROUGH TIPPO
MARCHING ON THE FOOTBALL FIELD
MONA MAE THE MAJORETTE
WHAT A POWER SHE DOES WIELD
SHE CAN MAKE THAT BATON
PUT ON QUITE A SHOW
AS MONA MAE GOES MARCHING ON
THROUGH TIPPO, TIPPO, TIPPO

MEN.   **WOMEN.** *(spoken)*

BRRUM-PUM, BRRUM-PUM
BRRR-RUM PUM!   TAKE IT MONA!

MONA.

MARCHING THROUGH TIPPO
HALFTIME OF THE GAME
LIFTING, LIFTING MY KNEES UP HIGH
TIPPO'S NEVER BEEN THE SAME!
SO PLAY THAT MARCHING SONG AGAIN
LET THE HEARTS OF AMERICA SWELL
I BRING TOGETHER MY COUNTRYMEN
FROM SUMMERFORD TO PATEL

(**COMPANY** *cheers as fanfares sound.*)

COMPANY. *(spoken)*

DO IT, MONA!

(**MONA** *performs baton tricks.*)

COMPANY. *(sung)*
> TWIRL IT…TOSS IT…CATCH IT…TURN IT…
> SPIN IT…SLIDE IT…GUIDE IT WHO KNOWS WHERE?
> FLIP IT…SLIP IT…STRUT IT…HIP IT…
> HOIST IT HIGHER, MONA, HIGHER, MONA,
> HIGHER, HIGHER, HIGHER
> GET IT UP, GET IT UP IN THE AIR!

MAVIS. Objection! Irrelevant male flashback fantasy.

JUDGE. Agreed! Nevertheless, overruled.

MAVIS. But Judge!

JUDGE. Overruled!!

MONA. *(As* **COMPANY** *hums softly)* Thank you, Your Honor. Ladies and gentlemen, I am Marching Through Tippo for a cause – Tippo has its own unique identity – armadillos and blues, gators and gospel – but a certain Queen of Mean wannabee would turn our town into a corporate-owned gambling mecca, where the only music heard will be the same stupid computer-generated melody, activated every time a senior citizen pulls the handle of a slot machine and blows his social security.
> THAT'S WHY I'M
> MARCHING THROUGH TIPPO
> MARCHING 'CAUSE I'M DADGUM MAD!

COMPANY. *(spoken)*
> THAT'S RIGHT!

MONA.
> CITIZENS, RALLY BEHIND ME

COMPANY.
> MONA!

MONA.
> RALLY TO SAVE THE FROG PAD!

COMPANY.
> YEAH!

MONA.
> CASINO CREEPS ARE GONNA LOSE
> IMAGINE THEIR LONG FACES
> WHEN THE FROG PAD'S
> ON THE NATIONAL REGISTER
> OF HISTORIC PLACES

MONA, McGNATS, COMPANY. *(spoken)*
RIBBIT, RIBBIT, ART EXHIBIT
FROG PAD, FROG PAD, RIBBIT RIBBIT RIBBIT!

MAVIS. *Your Honor!* I present Exhibit C, a copy of the Santa Claus Motel register for the night in question. Mr. Patel, show me the signatures of Mona Mae Katt and Euple R. Pugh.

PATEL. Here they are, Mr. And Mrs. John Philip Sousa.

MAVIS. You mean they didn't use their real names?

PATEL. Nobody is using their real names at the Santa Claus Motel. Ho! Ho! Ho!

MAVIS. Whose handwriting is this?

PATEL. It is looking like my handwriting.

MAVIS. Your Honor, there is no record of the defendant having been at the motel that night. This man's testimony is worthless!

JUDGE. I wouldn't say that, Ms. Frye. I do love a good march!

(Optional: Mona tuba solo)

COMPANY. *(sung)*
PLAY IT! TOOT IT! BLOW IT! HOOT IT!
SO PLAY THAT MARCHING SONG AGAIN
LET THE HEARTS OF AMERICA SWELL

MONA.	**COMPANY.**
I BRING TOGETHER	SHE BRINGS TOGETHER
MY COUNTRYMEN	HER COUNTRYMEN

MONA, COMPANY.
FROM SUMMERFORD – TO PUGH – TO PATEL!

(Song ends.)

JIM. *(To AUDIENCE)* I had to face facts – marching thru Tippo was exhilarating, but Mona's alibi was looking about as good now as a pom-pom stomped in the mud – and so was my case. I was desperate, I realized I had to appeal to the hearts of the jury. And for that I had to take my case to a higher court.
(To JUDGE) Your Honor, I'd like to present a special character witness –

MAVIS. A character witness? Jim Summerford, can't you do any better than that?

JIM. Your Honor, The Rev. Rosetta Purify, pastor of the Little Church Of Kingdom Come, and spiritual counselor to Mona Mae Katt.

MAVIS. This has nothing to do with the facts of the case. I object!

JUDGE. Overruled.

MAVIS. Why??!

JUDGE. Mavis…who wears the robe?

MAVIS. You do, Judge.

JUDGE. Rev. Purify also wears the robe! Bring on Rosetta!

CLERK. Raise your right hand and swear on the Bible.

REV. PURIFY. Brought my own stack.

CLERK. Well then, do you –

REV. PURIFY. I do, Amen. And Hallelujah, Brother.

CLERK. Hallelujah, Reverend, and praise his name.

REV. PURIFY. There is Power in the Blood!

CLERK. There is sunshine in my soul today.

REV. PURIFY. Shall we gather at the river!

CLERK. Wade in the water, children!

REV. PURIFY. He walks with me!

CLERK. And he talks with me! And he tells me I am his own! Oh! The joy we share, as we tarry there –

REV. PURIFY. That's enough! Bless you, that's enough! Thank you for testifying. Now I must give my testimony.

CLERK. Amen…

JIM. Amen! Reverend Purify, did you know C.C. Katt?

REV. PURIFY. That man had the devil in him. He stole the royalties from my church's gospel album, but even so, we prayed to forgive him.

JIM. Do you believe Mona did it?

REV. PURIFY. I do not, but half the town has already convicted her.

JIM. If you were giving a sermon right now to the people of Tippo, what would you say?

REV. PURIFY. Let my Mona go! It's all about forgiveness. Y'all done forgot, but the Bible says, God loves her, no matter what y'all think, and you know what . . .

COMPANY. What?

REV. PURIFY. Ain't none of y'all out there, amen –

COMPANY. Amen!

REV. PURIFY. Who ain't done bad sometime or the other, and now y'all try to put it all on her, try to make her the sacrificial lamb, amen –

COMPANY. Amen!

REV. PURIFY. Well you know what –

COMPANY. What?

REV. PURIFY. She ain't no lamb, hallelujah, and who amongst us is?

JIM. Hallelujah, Sister!

REV. PURIFY. Hallelujah, Jim!

CLERK. Hallelujah!

REV. PURIFY. Hallelujah, little buddy! Say Amen, somebody!

COMPANY. Amen, somebody –

REV. PURIFY. Well, all right –

SONG #16: YOU DONE FORGOT YOUR BIBLE

REV. PURIFY.
>NOW, WHO AMONG US
>HAS BEEN SINLESS AND SPOTLESS?

COMPANY.
>SINLESS AND SPOTLESS

REV. PURIFY.
>TIPPO IS HOT

COMPANY.
>HOT

REV. PURIFY.
>AND WHO HAS NOT

COMPANY.
>NOT

REV. PURIFY.
>GOTTEN INTO HOTNESS?

COMPANY.

GOTTEN INTO HOTNESS

REV. PURIFY.

JESUS MET THE WOMAN AT THE WELL AND THEN
HE FORGAVE MARY MAGDALEN'
AND THAT IS IN THE BIBLE
HAVE YOU DONE FORGOT YOUR BIBLE, HALLEY-LOO?

COMPANY.

FORGOT YOUR BIBLE, HALLEY-LOO

MAVIS. Objection!

(spoken) REVEREND,
(sung) THE GOD OF THE BIBLE
THE ONE WHO WROTE THE BOOK

COMPANY.

THE KING JAMES BOOK

MAVIS.

HE DESTROYED LOT'S WIFE

COMPANY.

BYE BYE WIFE

MAVIS.

AND ALL SHE DID WAS LOOK

COMPANY.

BETTER NOT LOOK

MAVIS.

AN EYE FOR AN EYE
A TOOTH FOR A TOOTH
YOU AND MONA CAN'T DENY
THAT'S THE GOD'S TRUTH
HAVE YOU DONE FORGOT YOUR BIBLE?
WELL, YOU DONE FORGOT YOUR BIBLE, HALLEY-LOO

COMPANY.

FORGOT YOUR BIBLE, HALLEY-LOO

REV. PURIFY.

NO, YOU DONE FORGOT YOUR BIBLE

REV. PURIFY, MAVIS.

YOU DONE FORGOT YOUR BIBLE

REV. PURIFY, MAVIS, COMPANY.

HAL-LEY-LOO...

(Double-time tempo)

COMPANY.

HALLEY-LOO…

REV. PURIFY.

JUDGE NOT, THAT YE BE NOT JUDGED
LET THE WOMAN WITHOUT SIN
CAST THE FIRST STONE

MAVIS.

BEHOLD A PALE HORSE, HIS NAME IS DEATH
THE WICKED WILL CRY, AND CRY ALONE

(Add **COMPANY** *background vocals/ OO-OO, WA-OO)*

REV. PURIFY.

TO SAVE ALL SINNERS, THAT IS HIS DESIRE

MAVIS.

NO, THE WICKED WILL BE CAST
INTO THE LAKE OF FIRE

REV. PURIFY.

FORGIVENESS, FORGIVENESS, IT'S ABOUT TIME

MAVIS.

PUNISHMENT, PUNISHMENT TO FIT THE CRIME

(COMPANY *background vocals out)*

REV. PURIFY, MAVIS.

WELL, YOU DONE FORGOT YOUR BIBLE
YOU DONE FORGOT YOUR BIBLE
YOU DONE FORGOT YOUR BIBLE, HALLEY-LOO-OO-OO

REV. PURIFY, COMPANY.

WELL, YOU DONE FORGOT YOUR BIBLE
YOU DONE FORGOT YOUR BIBLE

MAVIS, COMPANY.

YOU DONE FORGOT YOUR BIBLE, HALLEY-LOO-OO-OO

(COMPANY *vocals continue under* **MAVIS** *and* **REV. PURIFY** *)*

REV. PURIFY.

LET MY MONA GO

MAVIS.

NO, NO, NO, NO , NO

REV. PURIFY.

LET MY MONA GO

MAVIS.

NO, NO, NO, NO, NO

REV. PURIFY.

LET MY MONA GO

MAVIS.

NO, NO, NO, NO, NO

REV. PURIFY.

LET MY MONA

REV. PURIFY/MAVIS.

GO/NO, GO/NO, GO/NO

REV. PURIFY. (COMPANY *OO-OO, WA-OO*)

REMEMBER ON THE THIRD DAY, THE SAVIOUR ROSE

MAVIS.

REMEMBER THE SOLDIERS,
THEY GAMBLED FOR HIS CLOTHES

REV. PURIFY.

THE SON OF GOD DIED TO PAY OUR DEBT

MAVIS.

SAID HE WAS COMING BACK,
WE HAVEN'T SEEN HIM YET!

REV. PURIFY.

GOD MADE LIGHT OUT OF THE DARK
GAVE US ALL HIS DIVINE SPARK

MAVIS.

GOD GAVE SINNERS A PLACE TO DWELL
AND EVERY SINNER IS GOING TO –

REV. PURIFY, COMPANY.

WELL!

REV. PURIFY, MAVIS, COMPANY.

YOU DONE FORGOT YOUR BIBLE
YOU DONE FORGOT YOUR BIBLE
YOU DONE FORGOT YOUR BIBLE, HALLEY-LOO-OO-OO

YOU DONE FORGOT YOUR BIBLE
YOU DONE FORGOT YOUR BIBLE
YOU DONE FORGOT YOUR BIBLE, HALLEY-LOO

YOU DONE FORGOT YOUR BIBLE
YOU DONE FORGOT YOUR BIBLE, HALLEY-LOO!
HAL-LEY-LOO!!!!!
(Song ends.)

JIM. I got to hand it to you, Mavis. You just dueled God to a draw. You're some tough lawyer.

MAVIS. The sooner I win, the sooner we get married.

JIM. And honeymoon at your casino? Was C.C. Katt backing you all along?

MAVIS. Honey, I'm doing this for us. When I'm elected and the casino comes, you'll never have to try another case. And once one casino comes –

JIM. More casinos?

MAVIS. We could take over this state. We look right together, Jim. Have you thought of how important it is for a couple to look right together?

JIM. It never crossed my mind.

MAVIS. See? I really do know what's best. To show you how much I love you, I'm going to offer you a deal. Mona pleads guilty to Murder Two and I'll settle for three consecutive life sentences.

JIM. That's very generous of you, Mavis.

JUDGE. Mr. Summerford, do you wish to call another witness?

JIM. Your Honor, I'm all out of witnesses. A moment with my client, please?

JUDGE. *Just* a moment, Mr. Summerford. The court is waiting.

JIM. Mavis has offered us a plea. If we take it, you'll spend the rest of your life in prison. Or we can fight it to the end.

MONA. I won't plead guilty, because I didn't do it, Jim. I swear!

JIM. Mona, they're about to punch your ticket to Beulah Land. Blind Willy has placed you outside Star Studio at the time of the crime. They found your guitar and your wedding dress –

MONA. Why wasn't there any blood on my guitar, if I'm supposed to have done it? And that dress, I know I left it at the hotel! *(rapid-fire Spanish, blowing off steam)* Estoy tan cansada de todo esto, eres igual a ella, Dios Mío!

JIM. Now you tell me.

MONA. You believe me, don't you?

JIM. Yes...yes. I'm just confounded.

MONA. And you've never beaten Mavis.

JIM. I have a theory about that.

MONA. Oh? What is it?

JIM. She's a better lawyer. *(Music in, #17.)*

MONA. I couldn't disagree with you more! You're a fabulous lawyer, you've taken us a lot farther than I ever thought possible. I want to help you go the distance, Jim.

JIM. I need all the help I can get.

MONA. I have a theory about that.

JIM. You do?

SONG #17: PARTNER

MONA.

> ANYONE WHO'LL TELL YOU
> THEY'VE GOT ALL THE ANSWERS
> MUST NOT BE ASKING ENOUGH QUESTIONS
> NEWLY DEPARTED RECORD BIZ ROMANCERS
> COLD-HEARTED PROSECUTOR POLITICIANS
> BUT ANYONE WHO'LL TAKE
> ALL THE HELP THEY CAN GET
> AND GIVE IT IN RETURN, FOR STARTERS
> MIGHT BE SOMEONE
> FOR GOING DOWN THE ROAD WITH
> SOMEONE WHO COULD BE A PARTNER
>
> AND I THINK OF YOU THAT WAY, PARTNER
> MORE TODAY THAN YESTERDAY, PARTNER
> WHATEVER YOU'RE GOING THROUGH,
> WE'LL PUT OUR HEADS TOGETHER
> I KNOW ME PLUS YOU
> CAN ONLY MAKE IT BETTER
> IN DIFFERENT WAYS, EACH OF US IS SMARTER
> SO WHAT DO YOU SAY, PARTNER?
> WHAT DO YOU SAY, PARTNER?

JIM. Socio – ?

MONA. Sí, Socio!

> PIENSA ASÍ DE MÍ, SOCIO?

JIM.
 HOY MAS…QUE…

MONA. *(spoken)*
 AYER –

JIM. *(spoken)*
 AYER –

MONA, JIM. *(sung)*
 SOCIO!
 LO QUE ESTÁS SUFRIENDO
 LE DAREMOS SÓLUCION
 YO SÉ QUE TÚ Y YO
 SOLO PODREMOS MEJORARLO

JIM.
 EN DIFERENTES MANERAS,
 CADA UNO ES INTELIGENTE

MONA.
 ENTONCES DIME, SOCIO?

JIM.
 DIME, SOCIO!

MONA.
 QUÉ ME DICE, SOCIO?

JIM.
 DIME, SOCIO!

MONA.
 THE OUTCOME, NO ONE CAN GUARANTEE…

JIM.
 LO QUE SERÁ, SERÁ…

MONA.
 BUT YOU'LL ALWAYS

JIM.
 SIEMPRE –

MONA.
 MAKE PARTNER

JIM.
 SOCIO –

MONA, JIM.
 WITH ME!
 MI SOCIO!

 (Song ends.)

JIM. Mavis, no deal.

JUDGE. Ms. Frye, you ready for your summation?

MAVIS. You betcha, Your Honor. Ladies and gentlemen, Mona Mae Katt is guilty of murder. You've heard the evidence – ironclad. I urge you, vote to convict, and render the kind of swift justice the good people of Tippo deserve. Let Mona be an example, and her fate a deterrent to criminals everywhere. Law and order will be the hallmark of my tenure as Mayor – and then Governor – or my name isn't Frye.

JUDGE. Mr. Summerford?

SONG #18: A REAL DEFENSE

JIM.

LADIES AND GENTLEMEN, TODAY
YOU THE PEOPLE HAVE YOUR SAY
WITH ALL DUE DILIGENCE, YOU WEIGH THE EVIDENCE
FOR GUILT OR INNOCENCE

ON THE PERRY MASON SHOW
THIS IS THE MOMENT THAT WE WOULD KNOW
THE REAL KILLER WITH A ROAR
WOULD MAKE A RUN FOR THE DOOR

BUT I'M NOT RAYMOND BURR
THOUGH RIGHT NOW I WISH I WERE
I'D PUT ON THE EXTRA WEIGHT, IF IT'S NOT TOO LATE
TO SPRING A REAL DEFENSE FOR HER

COMPANY.

A REAL DEFENSE
A REAL DEFENSE
A REAL DEFENSE FOR HER!

JIM, (COMPANY).

SHE'S NOT GUILTY!
SHE'S AS INNOCENT AS SHE CAN BE (OOO-WAH!)
NOT OF LUST, NOT OF PRIDE,
BUT OF GUITAR HOMICIDE
MONA MAE MUST GO FREE!

COMPANY.

MUST GO FREE!

JIM, (COMPANY).
> SO DON'T LET HER BE A MARTYR (OOO-WAH!)
> IN THAT BODY THAT WON'T QUIT (OOO-WAH!)
> PLEASE, PLEASE DON'T DISCARD HER (OOO-WAH!)
> LIKE A DRESS THAT DOESN'T FIT (OOO-OOO-WAH!)
>
> WHAT WAS THAT I JUST SAID?
> THE THOUGHT THAT JUST WENT THROUGH MY HEAD
> HER BODY THAT WON'T QUIT
> HER BODY THAT WON'T QUIT
> A DRESS THAT DOESN'T FIT (FI – IT)
> A DRESS THAT DOESN'T FIT (FI – IT)
> A DRESS THAT DOESN'T FIT

JIM, COMPANY.
> A DRESS THAT DOESN'T FIT!

JIM. *(spoken)*
> THAT'S IT!
>
> *(Song ends, no applause; move immediately to scene, played at screwball speed.)*

JIM. Your Honor, I require Exhibit B – the dress!

MAVIS. Objection! He finished his summation!

JIM. The life of my client is at stake, Your Honor.

JUDGE. Overruled! Bring out Exhibit B!

> *(The DRESS is brought out in a plastic bag.)*

BAILIFF. Exhibit B, the Yoo-Hoo Dress!

JIM. *(To AUDIENCE)* Ladies and gentlemen, you heard testimony that everybody in town has one. As you can plainly see, (**JIM** *holds up DRESS, unfolded, next to* **MONA**.) this dress is nowhere near Mona's size!

COMPANY. *(in unison)* Holy cow!!!

JIM. *(To AUDIENCE)* The spectators went into an uproar – *(AUDIENCE reacts)*

> They got louder – (**JIM** *urges them on*) – And louder – *(AUDIENCE gets louder)*
>
> Until the Judge gavelled 'em down!

JUDGE. Order! Order!

MAVIS. Your Honor, this is preposterous!

JUDGE. Mr. Summerford –

JIM. Exhibit B is a completely different dress, planted at the scene of the crime by the real murderer. Whoever killed C.C. Katt hated Mona enough to frame her. Mavis, we've heard testimony that you had perfume just like Mona's, and a dress just like Mona's. Where is your dress, Mavis?

MAVIS. When I found out that Mona had the same dress, I gave mine to the Goodwill – and they'll be getting that perfume too.

JIM. Mavis Frye, I accuse you of the murder of C.C. Katt. Your Honor, my client should be released.

MAVIS. Jim Summerford, have you lost your tiny mind?!! Accusing me of murder, what will the voters think?!!!

JIM. Where were you on the night of July 1st at ten p.m.?

MAVIS. You fool, I was with you. It was my birthday!!

JIM. *(Groans)*

COMPANY. Nice groan.

JUDGE. Mr. Summerford, this one beats your Opening Statement.

JIM. *(To AUDIENCE)* But if the dress was not Mona's, where did it come from? I replayed in my mind what all the witnesses had said...

SONG #19: SPOOKY MEMORIES.

(WITNESSES appear in stylized lighting.)

TISH.
"THE BIG MEOW MADE US ALL A WRECK –
WRECK, WRECK!"

MONA. "Why was there no blood on my guitar?"

CORONER. "Rhonda's gums were blue"

BLIND WILLY. "I call it Eau de No Mercy"

PATEL. "It is looking like my handwriting"

MAVIS. "You fool, I was with you"

OFFICER BELL.
"BUT C.C. KATT NEVER WOULD GRANT ME AN
AUDITION"

REV. PURIFY. "That man had the devil in him"

JIM. Let me hear that other one again.

REV. PURIFY. "That man had the devil . . ."

JIM. *(cuts her off)* No, no, not that one.

OFFICER BELL.

". . . NEVER WOULD GRANT ME AN AUDITION"

JIM. But there was something else he said.

OFFICER BELL. "Hey Mona"

JIM. No, not that.

OFFICER BELL.

"I'M JUST TRYING TO BE HELPFUL . . ."

JIM. That's the one!

OFFICER BELL.

"HELPFUL . . ." *(Music out, under* **JIM.***)*

JIM. Your Honor, ladies and gentlemen of the jury, I'm not one of those clever attorneys we've all gotten used to. **(COMPANY** *mutters agreement.)* I'm just a small-town lawyer who still believes in the truth. And the truth is, if the real murderer doesn't come forward, it's going to ruin Mona's life, my life, the Frog Pad, and the Tippo we love. If we can't trust one another, if the best liar always wins, then Tippo becomes like everywhere else. Right now, I need everyone to be as helpful as possible. Officer Bell, this morning we spoke on the Courthouse steps. Could you please remind me – what kind of pizza did C.C. Katt have at his last meal?

BELL. Pepperoni!

JIM. Pepperoni, that's right. Yet no one in this trial ever mentioned the kind of pizza Katt was eating.

BELL. What?

JIM. The only way you could possibly know, Officer Bell, is because you were at Star Studio that night.

BELL. But . . .

JIM. What really went down, Bell? Do the right thing – sing out, Curly!

SONG #20: THE CONFESSION

BELL.
KATT SAID I SANG FLAT

JIM. *(spoken)*
SO?

BELL.
I MADE HIM A CADAVER

COMPANY.
OOO!

BELL.
I FRAMED MY MONA

JIM.
WHY?

BELL.
SO NO OTHER MAN COULD HAVE HER

COMPANY.
AAAHH!

JIM. But what about the dress?

BELL.
OH, THE GOODWILL WAS OPEN LATE

COMPANY.
LATE

BELL.
I MUST'VE BOUGHT MAVIS' DRESS

COMPANY.
YES!

BELL.
I POURED YOO-HOO ON IT

COMPANY.
(gasps)

BELL.
I -- I -- I -- CONFESS!
(Song ends.)

MONA. Wait a minute, he couldn't have killed Katt --

JIM. But he just confessed --

MONA. He intended to kill him, but look – there's no blood on the guitar – C.C.'s heart must have already stopped –

JIM. Officer Bell, where was Katt when you came into the studio?

BELL. On the floor.

JIM. Was he breathing?

BELL. I don't know, come to think of it – I just acted –

MONA. You bludgeoned him, but you didn't make him a cadaver – he already was a cadaver!

JIM. Officer Bell, you killed a dead man!

BELL. Oh, no! I killed a dead man. I killed a dead man??! That's awful! Is that a crime?

JUDGE. It's certainly tacky.

MAVIS. Would someone explain all this to the Prosecution? If Katt wasn't murdered by guitar, how was he killed?

MONA. Poison – !

JIM. Poison in the pizza!

MONA. The taste disguised by the pepperoni!

MAVIS. What do you know about it, anyway?

MONA. Handbook For Poisoners, Chapter Five: Cyanide can be made by boiling the leaves of the…what is it?

JIM. The laurel plant?

MONA. Yes, the laurel plant! But who else would know that?

JIM. Possibly an M.D. –

MONA. Or a D.D. –

CORONER. D. D. S.!!!

COMPANY. Dr. Bloodweather!

JIM. The laurel plants outside your office! You cooked up the cyanide!

CORONER. I was in love with Rhonda Zippers – then Katt made her one of his Kittens – I wanted to teach her a lesson, but only make her a little sick –

JIM. *You* made her gums turn blue –

CORONER. I went too far! And Katt knew! I had to kill him. He ruined my life.

MONA. So that night – ?

CORONER. Yes. I delivered the pizza. And I've delivered one last slice – to me!!!

JIM. Dr. Bloodweather – (*Music in,* **#20a** - *blaring guitar riffs*)

CORONER. Cyanide makes you jerk uncontrollably – (*more guitar*) But then I've always been a bit of a jerk – (*more guitar*) I did it for you, Rhonda! Help me Rhonda!! Help, help me Rhonda!!! I'M COMING RHONDA!!!!! (*spasmodic rocking guitar -* **CORONER** *falls dead theatrically - Music out.*)

JUDGE. Well, I must say, I've never had anyone die in my courtroom and in this trial we've had two bite the dust. It's certainly been interesting – however, I do declare this trial over! The Defendant is free to go!

JIM, MONA. We did it!! (**MONA & JIM** *embrace.*)

MAVIS. (*interrupts* **JIM**) Jim, oh, Jim? (*sincerely*) I thought you understood, I'm supposed to win! I always win!! Our engagement is off. I'm sorry for your pain. (*She walks away.*)

JUDGE. (*gavels*) Court is adjourned to the Frog Pad! (*Music in,* **#21**.)

JIM. Well, that's our story. Of course, a lot has happened in Tippo since the Trial – especially to some of the folks you met tonight. For example: (*gestures to* **JUDGE**)

JUDGE. Judge Ella Jordan is the star of her own TV Court Room Show, "No Hoochie, No Coochie."

PATEL. Mr. Johnny Patel, of the Santa Claus, now owns a string of motels across the South – The Dasher, The Dancer, The Prancer, and The Vixen. Ho! Ho! Ho!

BELL. Officer Bell arrested himself for killing a dead man, and while in jail recorded an album, "Officer Bell Sings a Few Bars Behind Bars."

TISH. Tish Thomas became a crime reporter and cabaret critic for The New York Times. (*Music out.*)

McGNATS. The McGnats were discovered by Ethan and Joel Coen. And starred in their latest hit ... "Oh, Tippo, Where Art Thou?" (*Music in - faster tempo.*)

MAVIS. Mavis Frye relocated to Biloxi, Mississippi, where she is CEO of Riverboat Total Care Casino, a pioneer in assisted gambling.

JIM. My new fiancée, Ramona María Katt, is running unopposed for Mayor.

COMPANY. Yay! Hooray! You go, Mona! *(variously)*

MONA. Hola, my little angels!

JIM. I'm still a lawyer. *(All react skeptically.)* But I'm also Director of the Tourism and Visitor's Bureau, and Chairman of our annual Frog Fest, which is growing by leaps and bounds. *(if they groan)* Nice groan.

JUDGE. Ms. Katt, Mr. Summerford, people of Tippo – it is my privilege to present this plaque, commemorating the Frog Pad as the oldest continuing juke joint in Georgia, now on the National Register Of Historic Places.

MONA. Thank you, Your Honor. Friends, we invite you to get out your roadmaps and pay us a visit.

JIM. There's a brand new walking tour of all the hot spots of the murder trial.

MONA. Stop by the Frog Pad after your tour, quench your thirst, relax, and enjoy some good ol' Tippo tunes.

JIM. Come and stay for a while. We'll be mighty glad to see you.

SONG #21: COME ON DOWN TO TIPPO

ALL.
 COME ON DOWN TO TIPPO TOWN
 TAKE THE MURDER TOUR

MAVIS.
 SEE THE STUDIO AT STAR

MONA.
 THE AFTER-DEATH GUITAR

ALL.
 WITH MONA MAE'S GLITTER SIGNATURE!

JUDGE.
 THE PINK CADILLAC
 IS MOUNTED ON THE ROOF

JUDGE, MAVIS.
 OF THE EUPLE R. PUGH SCHOOL OF LAW

PATEL.

STAY WITH MR. PATEL AT THE SANTA CLAUS MOTEL

ALL

GO HOME AND TELL 'EM ALL WHAT YOU SAW!
TIPPO TOWN, COME ON DOWN

OFFICER BELL.

SCENE OF THE CRIME

ALL.

HAVE YOURSELF A LA-ARGE TIME
DON'T YOU KNOW
ALL ROADS LEAD TO TIPPO – O
COME ON DOWN
COME ON DOWN
COME ON DOWN TO TIPPO!
COME ON DOWN
COME ON DOWN
COME ON DOWN TO TIPPO!

(**CAST** *takes bows as music continues.*)

ALL.

TIPPO TOWN, COME ON DOWN
SCENE OF THE CRIME
HAVE YOURSELF A LA-ARGE TIME
DON'T YOU KNOW
ALL ROADS LEAD TO TIPPO-O
COME ON DOWN
COME ON DOWN
COME ON DOWN TO TIPPO!
COME ON DOWN
COME ON DOWN
COME ON DOWN TO TIPPO!

(*Song ends.* **ALL** *wave to AUDIENCE.* **CAST** *exits.*
McGNATS *play Exit Music - "McGnat's Mayhem" - and
exit.*)

THE END

Also by
Jim Wann...

Diamond Studs

Gold Dust

Hot Grog

King Mackerel & the Blues Are Running

Pump Boys and Dinettes

Please visit our website **samuelfrench.com** for complete descriptions and licensing information